GRANDMA'S PURSE

Vanessa Brantley-Newton

Alfred A. Knopf
New York

Today my grandma Mimi is coming to visit. When Mimi comes over, she always has a new treasure to share.

And no matter what it is, it comes from inside her purse.

I can't look away from it! It must be full of some magical things. All of the things that make my grandma Mimi.

"Will you show me what's inside?"

Yes, she will!

"I keep all kinds of things in my purse. You never know what you'll want to have with you!"

"I use my mirror to see myself before you see me. I use it to put on my lipstick so my lips are ready to give you a big kiss!"

"And you have your smell-good!"
Mimi laughs. "Yes. I use my smell-good so
you know I was here even after I go home."

"I keep extra earrings in my purse in case
I want to feel extra-fancy."

"And my hairpins keep
my hair just so."

"This coin purse holds my coins, of course, but it also holds memories. Your grandfather brought it back from Japan for me. So when I do something small like put away change, I do something big and think of him, too."

"Candy!!"

"You never know when you'll need a little treat!"

Mimi always passes me a piece of candy to suck on in church,

right when I start having a hard time paying attention to the pastor.

"Your phone looks like a toy."

"It has my friends' phone numbers on it— what else would I need it for?!"

"My glasses help me see your pretty face. And this scarf can keep me warm, or give me a cushion if I want to rest my head, or it can make me feel fancy if my earrings don't do it on their own."

So this is how Mimi gets to be Mimi. With everything in her purse, I can be Mimi, too!

Toward the bottom of the bag, I find a sleeve of pictures.
At first I only recognize one—me! But Mimi shows me who's in
the others. There's Mimi a long time ago when she married Papa,
and another of my mom when she was my age.

She looks like me! Only without all of Mimi's accessories.

There's one more thing
at the very bottom.

I couldn't see it until we took out
all of Mimi's treasures, one by one.

It's big, and it has my
name on it.

A purse of my own!

And I know what will go in first.

For my Gullah Geechee Belles,
who carried history in their pocketbooks

Educators and librarians, for a variety of teaching tools, visit us at RHTeachersLibrarians.com

Visit us on the Web! rhcbooks.com

Library of Congress Cataloging-in-Publication Data is available upon request.
ISBN 978-1-5247-1431-4 (trade) — ISBN 978-1-5247-1432-1 (lib. bdg.) — ISBN 978-1-5247-1433-8 (ebook)

The text of this book is set in 20-point Julius Primary Bold.
The illustrations were created using gouache and charcoal pencil on watercolor paper, Corel Painter, and Adobe Photoshop.

MANUFACTURED IN CHINA

January 2018   10 9 8 7 6 5 4 3 2 1   First Edition